Hamish McHaggis

This book belongs to

....

....

GW Publishing

Hamish

This is Hamish the haggis
of the McHaggis clan,
rarely seen by
the eyes of man.

Rupert Harold the Third
is an English gent,
travelling far from
his home in Kent.

Rupert

Our Jeannie's an osprey with wide sweeping wings,
who is easily distracted by all sorts of things.

Jeannie

Angus

Young Angus is cheeky and likes playing the fool,
whatever he's doing, he's got to look cool.

For Sarah
with love. L.S.

In fond memory of my father-
my inspiration for Hamish. S.J.C.

Text and Illustrations copyright © Linda Strachan and Sally J. Collins

www.lindastrachan.com
www.hamishmchaggis.co.uk

First Published in paperback in Great Britain 2005
Reprinted 2007, 2009, 2012 and 2015

Design - Veneta Altham

Reprographics - GWP Graphics

Printed in China

Published by

GW Publishing
PO Box 15070
Dunblane
FK15 5AN
Scotland

www.gwpublishing.com

ISBN 09546701-7-5
978-0-9546701-7-7

Hamish McHaggis

and

The Edinburgh Adventure

By Linda Strachan

Illustrated by Sally J. Collins

squawk!
squawk!

Hamish McHaggis
The McHaggis Hoggle
Coorie Doon
Highland Glen

It was a bright morning in Coorie Doon.
Hamish McHaggis opened the front door of his
Hoggle and stood enjoying the sunshine. Pigeon the
Postie flew down and dropped a letter at his feet.

"Special Delivery!" he squawked.

Hamish did a jig in delight. "They've arrived," he
garbled through a mouthful of toast.

"Look!" Hamish wheezed as he climbed up the hill.
"They've just arrived in the post."
Rupert looked up from his paper. "What's that?"
"Tickets for the Edinburgh
Tattoo." Hamish stopped to catch
his breath and waved the tickets
in front of Rupert's nose.

"Can we all go?" asked Angus.

"Of course," said Hamish. "I've got four tickets."

"I can't wait to go to Edinburgh."

"There'll be fireworks and marching bands."

"Jugglers and clowns
on the street."

"I want to get
some bagpipes."

The next day they set off for Edinburgh
in the Whirry-Bang. They were all enjoying the
trip and singing Hamish's favourite song, Ally Bally
Bee, when suddenly there was

a loud

bang

and a

crunch

and the Whirry-Bang tipped to one side.
"Help ma Boab!" cried Hamish. "The wheel's come off."

crunch!
Bang!

"What are we going to do?" asked Rupert.
Hamish opened the picnic basket and helped
himself to a sandwich. "I can fix it," he said, "but
we'll need to get to Edinburgh first."

"How are we going to get there without a wheel?" asked Angus.
"I have an idea," Hamish told him.

"I know how we can get a lift to Edinburgh,"
Hamish grinned.

Parked in front of them was a huge
car-transporter. Hamish ran over and
jumped onto the back of it. "If we can
get the Whirry-Bang up here, we can
get a lift to Edinburgh."

"I've got a rope," Rupert
said, pulling a coil of strong rope
out of the back of the Whirry-Bang.
He tied it on tightly to the front.

Jeannie pulled on the rope
and everyone else pushed as
hard as they could. With a...

heave

and a

shove...

...they pushed the Whirry-Bang up
onto the back of the car-transporter.

Before long they had arrived in Edinburgh.

"Wow! There's the castle!" Jeannie fluttered her wings.

"That's where they hold the Tattoo," Hamish told Rupert.
"Up there where all the flags are, in front of the castle."

"Can we go up there now?" Angus jumped up and down
on the spot.
          "Can we?
                    Can we?"

"Don't get yer semmit in a fankle,
Angus," Hamish told him. "We have to
get the Whirry-Bang fixed first."

"Ah, I know that one," announced
Rupert, with a grin. "A semmit... that's
a vest, isn't it?"

"Can't we go exploring?" Angus whined. "I'm bored."

"Angus and I could go and have a look around while you fix the wheel," Rupert suggested.

"Good idea," Jeannie nodded.
"We won't be too long."
    So Jeannie and Hamish started
working on the Whirry-Bang. She
flew about handing him the tools
he needed to fix the wheel.

Rupert and Angus set off towards Princes Street Gardens. There was a bandstand with music playing and lots of people sitting about on the grass in the sunshine.

"Look, Rupert. There are some dancers and jugglers! That looks fun!"

"Let's go and have a look at the fountain over there. Stay close, Angus," Rupert warned him, "you might get lost."

"I never get lost!" Angus said, with a cheeky smile. "I always know where I am!"

But a few minutes later, when Rupert looked for him, Angus was nowhere to be seen.

Rupert went back to tell Hamish and Jeannie that Angus was missing. "One moment he was there and the next he had gone," Rupert said, looking miserable.

"Don't worry, Rupert," Jeannie patted him gently. "We'll find him. Let's get on that bus. We can see better from up there."

When the bus came around the front of the new Scottish Parliament building Hamish gave a shout. "Look, there he is. Let's get off here."

They jumped off the bus, but they couldn't see Angus anymore.

"Let's go up the Royal Mile, towards the castle. He might have gone there," Jeannie suggested. Hamish was beginning to feel tired and hungry when Rupert gave a shout.

"Look There he is!"

Angus was in front of a crowd of people with a troupe of jugglers. When he finished juggling he got a round of applause and gave a little bow. "That was fun" he grinned.

"Oh look, bagpipes. I always wanted to try them."
Rupert blew into the bagpipes and they made a
strange screeching noise.

Hamish covered his ears. "Gie us a breke, Rupert!"

"Perhaps I need a bit of practice!"

Shaking his head, Hamish set off for the castle to
find their seats for the Tattoo.

Wow!

¡Qué bonito!

Bello!

La Belle Rouge!

As it got dark they settled down to watch the Tattoo. There were marching bands, dancers and a motorbike display team doing dangerous stunts. At the end there was the lone piper playing his bagpipes up on the battlements, followed by an amazing show of fireworks that lit up the night sky.

DID YOU KNOW?

Coorie Doon means to nestle or cosy down comfortably.

Blether means to gossip or chatter.

"Help ma Boab!" is an exclamation of surprise.

Gie us a breke means stop doing something (give us a break from it).

Don't get yer semmit in a fankle means don't get all worked up or too excited about something.

Haggis It is commonly thought that a Haggis has three legs, two long and one short. Hamish thinks this is highly amusing!

Semmit means vest.

Fankle means tangle.

Can you find me on each page?

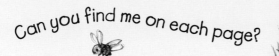

Angus is a Pine Marten.

Pine Martens are mainly found north of the Great Glen.

Hedgehogs dislike bright light and prefer to come out at night.

Ospreys build their nests made of sticks at the top of high trees.

The Royal Mile is a road a mile long that goes from Holyrood Palace and the new Scottish Parliament, all the way up to Edinburgh Castle.

Edinburgh is the capital city of Scotland.

The Edinburgh Tattoo takes place in August and September every year, during the Edinburgh International Festival.

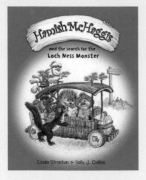

**Hamish McHaggis
and The Search for The
Loch Ness Monster**

978-0-9546701-5-3

**Hamish McHaggis
and The Edinburgh Adventure**

978-0-9546701-7-7

**Hamish McHaggis
and The Ghost of Glamis**

978-0-9546701-9-1

**Hamish McHaggis
and The Skye Surprise**

978-0-9546701-8-4

**Hamish McHaggis
and The Skirmish at Stirling**

978-0-9551564-1-0

**Hamish McHaggis
and The Wonderful Water Wheel**

978-0-9551564-0-3

**Hamish McHaggis
and The Wonderful Water Wheel**

978-0-9554145-5-8

**Hamish McHaggis
and The Clan Gathering**

978-0-9561211-2-7

**Hamish McHaggis
and The Great
Glasgow Treasure Hunt**

978-0-9570844-0-7

**Hamish McHaggis
Activity and Story Book**

978-0-9554145-1-0

Also by the
same author
and illustrator

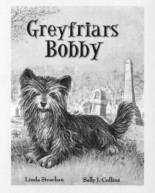

Greyfriars Bobby

978-0-9551564-2-7